The WATER CYCLE

Nicolas Brasch

Australia • Brazil • Japan • Korea • Mexico • Singapore • Spain • United Kingdom • United States

The Water Cycle

Fast Forward
Green Level 12

Text: Nicolas Brasch
Illustrations: Luke Jurevicius
Editor: Johanna Rohan
Design: Stella Vassiliou
Series design: James Lowe
Production controller: Emma Hayes
Photo research: Gillian Cardinal
Audio recordings: Juliet Hill, Picture Start
Spoken by: Matthew Hill, Abbe Holmes

Acknowledgements
The author and publisher would like to acknowledge permission to reproduce material from the following sources: Photographs by istockphoto/Diane Diederich, p. 6 bottom Lise Gagne, p. 6 centre/Sami Suni, p. 8 right/Christopher Ermel, pp. 14, 23 top left/Nathan Goodman, pp. 18, 23 top right, back cover; Photolibrary.com/Alaska Stock Images, front cover, pp. 1, 4-5, 7/Untitled, pp. 4, 16/Photonica, pp. 8, 14 -15/Peter Arnold Images,
p. 9/Reso EEIG, p. 12/Veer, pp. 13, 22/Botanica, pp. 23 bottom right, 27/© Andrew Penner/iStockphoto, pp. 18-19/Bildhuset Ab, p. 20 /Imagestate Ltd, pp. 21, 23 bottom left.

ISBN 978 0 17 012568 0
ISBN 978 0 17 012561 1 (set)

Cengage Learning Australia
Level 7, 80 Dorcas Street
South Melbourne, Victoria Australia 3205
Phone: 1300 790 853

Cengage Learning New Zealand
Unit 4B Rosedale Office Park
331 Rosedale Road, Albany, North Shore NZ 0632
Phone: 0800 449 725

For learning solutions, visit **cengage.com.au**

Printed in Australia by Ligare Pty Ltd
9 10 11 12 13 14 15 19 18 17 16 15

THE UNIVERSITY OF MELBOURNE

Evaluated in independent research by staff from the Department of Language, Literacy and Arts Education at the University of Melbourne.

Nicolas Brasch

Contents

Chapter 1

THE WATER CYCLE

The process by which water moves from Earth to the sky and then back to Earth is called the water cycle.

Rain falls from the sky,
but it does not start its life in the sky.
Rain starts its life on Earth.
Water **vapour** rises into the air
and falls back on to Earth as rain.

During the water cycle, water takes three different forms:

- **liquid**
- **gas**
- **solid**.

The liquid form of water is rain, rivers, lakes and the ocean.

As a gas, water is called vapour.
As a solid,
water is called ice, snow and hail.

During the water cycle, water keeps changing its form over again.

Chapter 2

STAGES

There are four stages in the water cycle:

1. evaporation
2. condensation
3. precipitation
4. runoff.

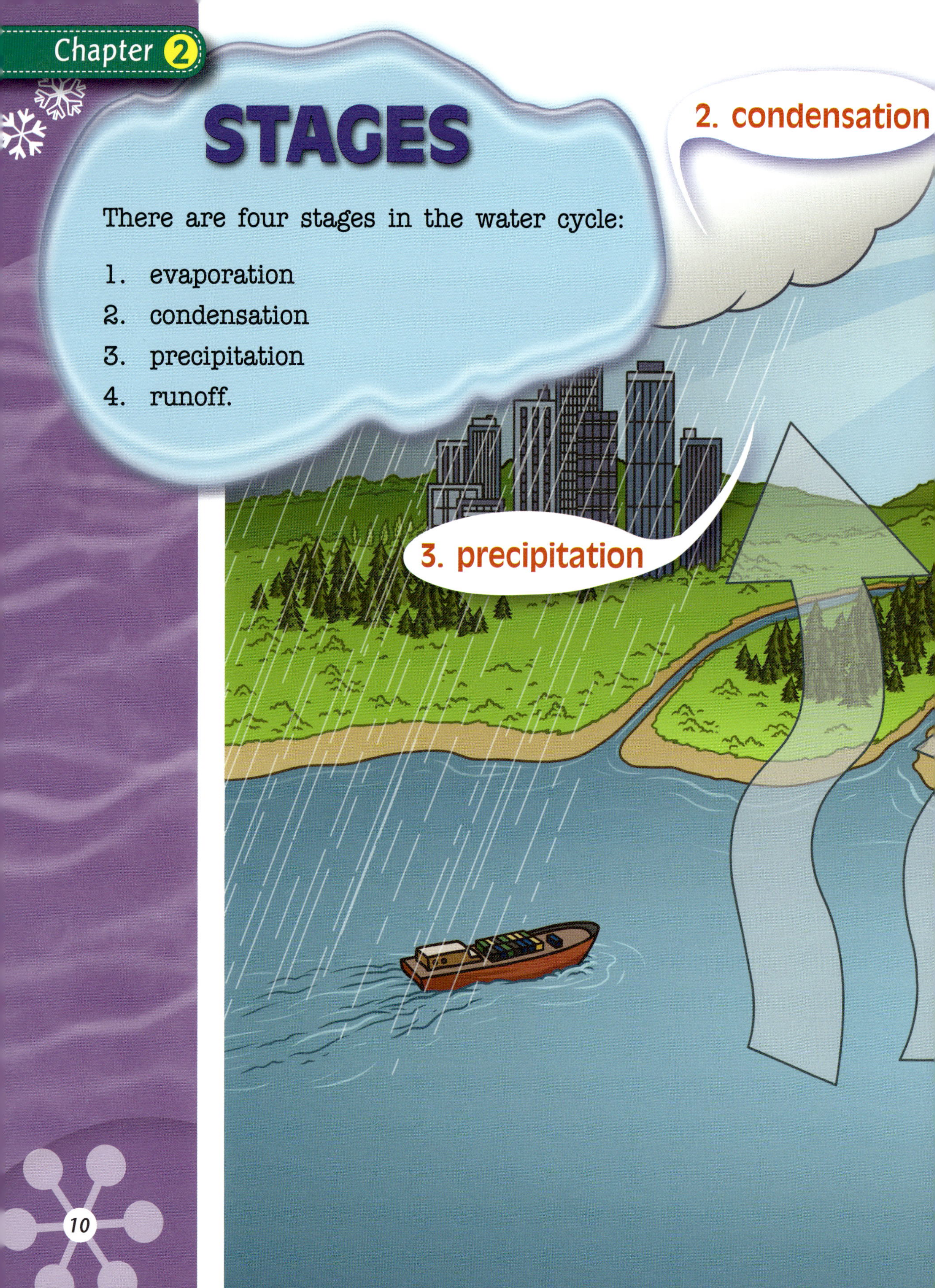

4. runoff
1. evaporation

EVAPORATION

The first stage of the water cycle is evaporation. Evaporation is when water changes from a liquid into a gas called vapour. This happens as a result of the Sun heating up the water.

Running Words 154

Vapour rises to the sky to form clouds because gases are lighter than air.

Chapter 4

CONDENSATION

The second stage of the water cycle is condensation.
Clouds hold water in the form of vapour.
The wind blows clouds across land and the ocean.
As clouds cool, condensation changes water from a gas to little drops of liquid.

Chapter 5

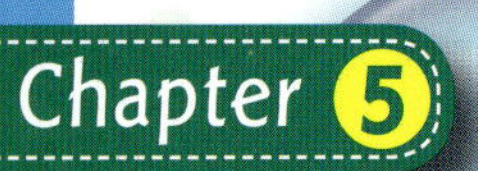

PRECIPITATION

The third stage of the water cycle is precipitation.
Precipitation is when the liquid in the sky falls to Earth.
This happens because the little drops of water join together to form bigger drops.

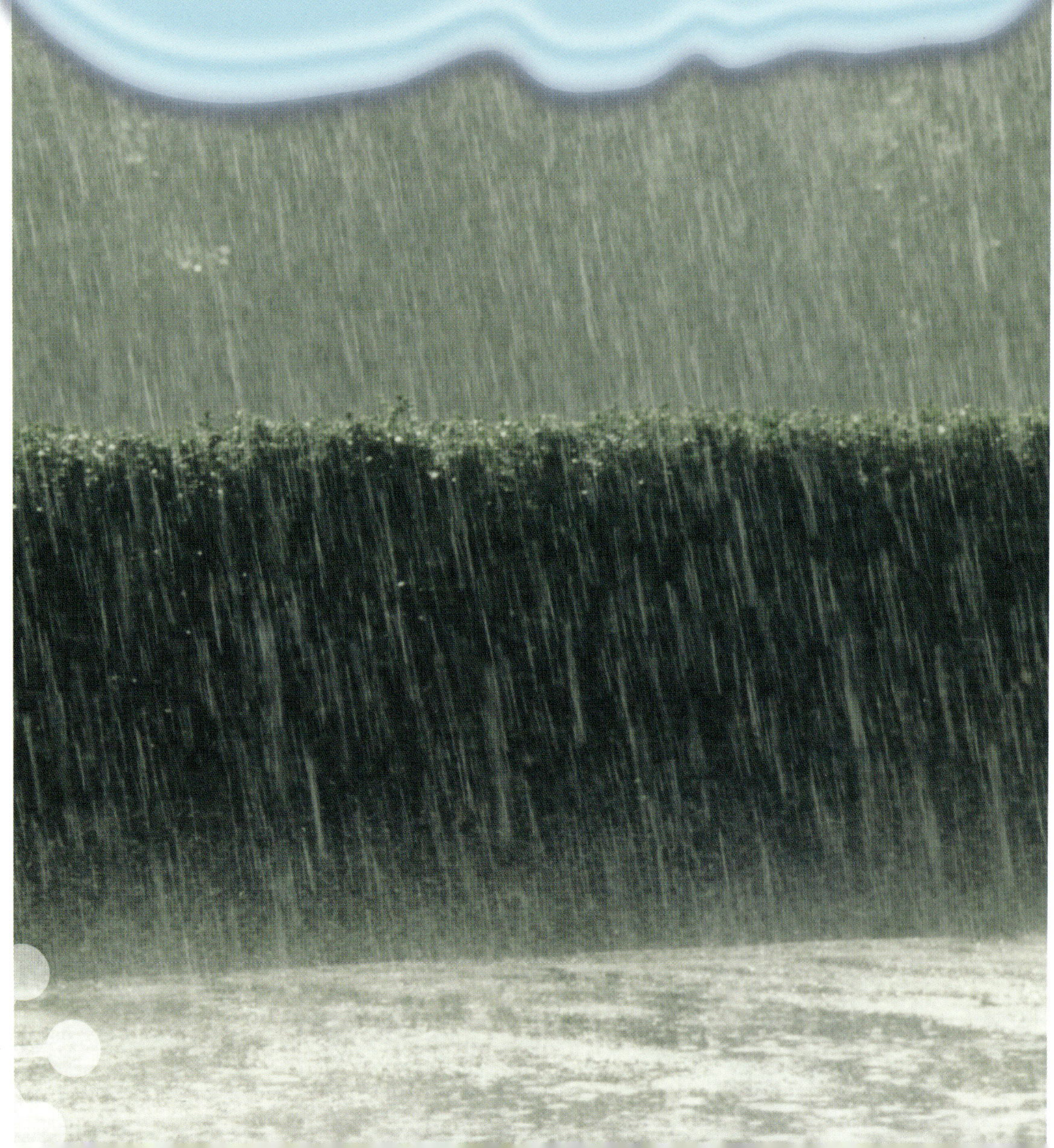

These drops of water
become too heavy to stay in the air,
so they fall to Earth as rain.

Precipitation is not always a liquid. Precipitation can sometimes fall in the form of a solid, like hail. This happens after very cold air has frozen the liquids into solids.

Then, these solids become too heavy to stay in the air, so they fall to Earth as hail or snow.

RUNOFF

The fourth stage of the water cycle is runoff. Runoff is when the rain that has fallen to Earth runs down a hill to form rivers and then into a lake or ocean.

Runoff also happens when hail or snow melts into a liquid and runs into a lake or the ocean.

Chapter 7

SUMMARY

1. Rain starts as a liquid in the ocean or a lake.
2. It is then heated and changed into a gas, called vapour.
   Vapour rises to the sky to form clouds.

3. As clouds cool, the vapour forms a liquid again.
4. The liquid becomes too heavy to stay in the air so it falls to Earth.
   Sometimes, it turns into a solid before falling.
5. The liquid runs back into the ocean or a lake.

The process then begins all over again.

Glossary

gas an air-like substance

liquid a substance that flows freely

solid a substance that is firm and has a fixed shape

vapour a gas such as mist or steam

Index